Celtic Mist:

Poems, Follies & Reflection

by

Rick Dail

Table of Contents

Poems

Follies

Reflection

Poems

O The Vessels of Life

Ships that sail,

Ships that dock,

Carrying hidden cargo stock.

Travel weathered seas,

For every distant land,

Some sailing, some wrecked upon the sand.

Times of glory,

Times of mutiny,

Adventures on the mild and the stormy seas.

Man surfs waves of time to know his destiny.

Ocean of Life

Oh, tempting ocean

Why do you hound my soul with the call of the wild,
Of sin, and tantalizing adventures and excitement,

Which tears my soul from reassuring solid ground,
And casts my fate into the unknown brine.

What is your mission howling sea?
Who bids you here?

For it is not I who desires your phantom-nous winds
Which heckles and chatters like shadows behind my back.

The conscience of my soul wearies of your lusts and sees,
Only Hope as strong enough to cut your intemperate winds.

I cast you out, yet you persist!

What drives your madness, the flames of hot hate,
You display at your leisure to torment mankind?

What is this...the howling stop?!

Perhaps your lustful hunger abates by the doom of still
another sadly doomed and cursed vessel.

Yet...how long, before you thirst for blood again?

###

Ode to Kevin Burns

They buried him up Michigan way,
They buried him on Valentine Day.

It's only fitting I suppose,
As he was love and they were cold.

Great the loss they failed to know,
Love now hidden by Northern snow.

It's only fitting I suppose,
Treasure is hidden like purest gold.

His heart was big as Texas,
Yet the world... it, they rejected.

It's only fitting I suppose,
They cannot miss what they've not known.

Great their loss I do believe,
A gem for free, they would not receive.

###

A Friend's Poem

A friend is loyal to you through thick and thin,
And a friend never leaves you alone.

A friend thinks about you all of the time,
With a friend you are not on your own.

A friend is someone whether far or near,
Who holds you up in prayers so dear.

A friend loves you for who you really are,
And sends you blessings from near and from afar.

A friend knows you are special in so many ways,
And values your thoughts and the words that you say.

A friend sees your heart and character each day,
And thanks God for His fruits you truly display

A friend is a copy of the Christ of The Way,
Who stands by your side by night and by day.

And Christ is the ultimate friend to us all,
He is faithful and true to us whenever we call.

And from Him our souls and our hearts receive rest.
For our future He plans will surely be the best.

So, we are of good cheer and nary perplexed,
Because He holds our future, one of peace and of rest!

The Kid Song

I don't wanna grow up,
I don't wanna grow up,
I just-want-to-be-a-child!

I don't wanna grow up,
I don't wanna grow up,
If it-means-I'll-loose-my-smile!

I don't wanna grow up,
I don't wanna grow up,
If the-sun-shine-goes-away!

I don't wanna grow up,
I don't wanna grow up,
If my-heart-must-turn-to-clay!

I don't wanna grow up,
I don't wanna grow up,
If my-dreams-don't-turn-out-true!

I don't wanna grow up,
I don't wanna grow up,
If my-hope-can't-be-renewed!

I don't wanna grow up,
I don't wanna grow up,
If my-friends-must-go-a-far!

I don't wanna grow up,
I don't wanna grow up,
If it means-I'll-go-to-war

I don't wanna grow up,
I don't wanna grow up,
It should-be-against-the-law!

Twas A Month Before Christmas

Twas a month before Christmas, the turkeys still kickin'.
Rick walked through the door, with a bucket of chicken.

Tired from the shopping, frazzled from noise,
His bag held a bundle, of trinkets and toys.

He poured them all out, on the couch and on the rug
When he started wrapping, shouted "Oh, HUMBUG!"

The paper too twisty, the tape did not stick
The bows were too bowey, it all made him sick!

What happened to Christmas, from when he was a child?
It was never this hurried, it was never this wild.

Twas a week before Christmas, what would he do?
There was so much more shopping and he had the flu.

He jumped from his bed and flew through the air
The sales were all starting and he must be there.

He smiled at the people, who wished him good cheer,
All he really wanted was his recliner and a beer.

It was this time of year that made him to think,
For he had no chair and he didn't drink!

He was ready to quit, he was glad to be done,
It was time to sit back, to see if Santa would come.

Twas Christmas Day, there was no time to pout,
Must bring down the presents and put them all out.

Smooth out the paper and fluff up the bows,
Wake up the kids by tickling their nose.

Once Rick heard the 'oohs' and 'aahs' and the screams,
He smiled as he thought what Christmas does mean.

His bank overdrafted, his cards overdue
For Christmas his bonus was a cookie or two.

So now it's all over, all have gone home
For the first time in ages, Rick was alone.

He heard from the courtyard a curious clatter.
But he didn't get up because it didn't matter!

Oh...Bah!! HUMBUG!

###

Water Meets Fire: A Prose Poem

The water was here; it had always been here in the deep
cool vastness of the abyss.

Undisturbed, its tranquil eddies had flowed through time
eternal in the dark unknown in aquatic bliss.

All the water had ever known was darkness,
And the endless march of time and peace.

Behold! Now it was different, an intruder had broken the
Serenity of water's world momentarily causing it to cease.

From the reaches somewhere up above a small glowing,
Ember had fallen into the abyss and rested in the corner.

What could this mean; from where did this invader come?
The water first anxiously desired to snuff out the foreigner,

Who most discourteously broke into its tranquil home.
Yet what harm had it really done?

Resolved that there was no duress or such great threat,
Water turned back to its endless and timeless roam.

Thus, such is how they came to co-exist,
Water on one side and the fire on the other.

Side by side with peacefulness restored,
In the abyss the twain reside opposite one another.

Time wearily dragged by passing off into eternity,
Each more relaxed at their strange existence together.

So harmonious did they co-exist that water didn't notice the
Flames that leaped up from the embers like fiery feathers.

Fire's intensity slowly and steadily grew hotter and fiercer,
The flames grew intense, fire could no longer be contained.

Fire began to spread, slowly at first, then in bursts,
The flaming inferno could no longer be restrained,

Fiery tongues that licked out into the cavern and dried up
the edges and eddies of water's pools.

Water, in horror, realized the ravaging flames were out of
control and could not be contained and could not be ruled.

Fire's singing tongues brought violent smoke, ash and heat,
Before long the fiery jaws snapped at water's main stream.

And at long last water's rippling currents coiled to fight,
The ensuing battle marked by crackle and the hiss of steam.

The flicker of light with clouds of vapor filling the cavern,
When the smoke had cleared the water had been victorious.

The seemingly unquenchable cauldron vanquished,
The flames were gone and water's achievement glorious.

At long last water settled back into its endless ebb and flow,
Idling again off into timeless tranquility ever so slow.

###

The Blessings of Solitude

When I was young I was constantly thinking,
Thoughts whirled in my head till it would almost explode.

Thoughts of folks, places and things sent my heart sinkin',
My thoughts turned to feelings and became quite a load.

Some feelings heavy and some feelings were quite light,
Feelings of joy and sorrow and some were of plain fear.

Feelings to the left and feelings to the right,
Feelings horrific and others precious and so very dear.

A slave to my feelings, they mastered my soul,
They consumed my energy, my time and my affairs.

They drove me to action to run far from my woe,
I ran to the shadows of folks I hoped might really care.

Exhausted and lonely and often confused,
Devoid of grace and peace, I was never at ease.

Feelings demand action and they made me feel used,
No matter the cost I always had others I just must please.

I lived life external; and empty and shallow and alone,
I thought "this is not normal", I just can't go on this way.

And dark and deep in the dead of the night, on my own,
I sensed a whisper of comfort, a spirit I might dare say.

A voice of a spirit so holy and true,
A whisper of someone that I recalled from the past.

It was the voice of Jesus, a person I already knew,
And He said you can "Trust Me" I'm your friend to the last.

So now I have peace and my thoughts are more tame,
I relax in Him knowing He always has my back.

Worry not I by waves of troubles nor torrents of shame,
Now I know I'm not forsaken if under attack.

My feelings are calmed and I sleep well at night,
I sail life's seas with courage, my soul is set free.

I know that I know my friend will always do whats right,
And no matter the test my friend is always faithful to me.

This Hallowed Ground Revisited

I stood in the meadow and looked far across the way.
I almost heard bugles wafting on the warm Spring wind,
And and the rumble of guns set to open the battle again
The farmland. the guardian of momentous past days.

I reflect on the struggles of men who answered the call,
In their time of duty put life on the line, rose up to serve,
Now denied by their descendants the respect they deserve,
Earned on this bloodsoaked soil where thousands did fall.

It's easy to judge bygone years from our armchairs today,
It's disingenuous to discount the times of countrymen past,
Yet, profit from the taxes, tears and blood spent to the last,
Instead, we should ask what price are we willing to pay?

We sit at leisure and judge yesterday like we are some God,
Lo, when we argue from general to specific and back again.
We make errors in logic and reason and ignorantly sin,
We compare apples to oranges like foolish, unwitting clods.

We cannot know the hearts of citizens we never knew,
If we solemnly refuse American dead dignity and respect,
What future can we really expect for such great neglect?
We judge men, yet we never walked a mile in their shoes?

This Earth purified with men's red blood.
History serves as witness against us with a cold stern glare,
To curse us who dishonor our own and should best beware,
To condemn us for dragging our fathers through the mud.

And so, on this field we stand on holy and sacred ground,
And should we judge history, history will in turn judge us,
If we trash history it's verdict on us may be harsh and just.
Let's pay homage to America's dead, let our glory abound!

Triple Citizenship

I was born in D. C. but it wasn't my fault,
A man without a country is what I've been told,
All I really remember is the cold, snow and the salt,
A war baby son, I left there when I was three years old,

We idled down South to find us some sun,
Not sure why, but I guess we were just living right!
Folks say I'm a traitor, but me, I be just a son of a gun,
Please tell the last one to leave to turn out the lights!

Daddy was from Carolina, where "nothing could be finer",
What they are talking about I think that I now know.
The old folks worked hard they had no time for whiners,
They got there early before the state or a Tobacco Row.

They sunk roots deep in the country before there was one,
Surely you catch my drift and I hope you will agree,
It's simply a great honor to be called a Southern's son.
So, I claim Southern citizenship, proudly, as it ought to be!

My mom was from Texas a "whole 'nother country" it be,
So there lives my exes, and some of my chillins and grands.
Grand pappy Slay paved the way, with a land grant in 1853,
Not born there but I did "get there as quick as I can".

A semi-centennial, and alumni of old Sam Houston State,
So don't mess with Texas, don't you dare give me no bull,
You too can migrate to Texas if you go before it's too late,
A Lone Star citizen, got scars to prove it, without any pull.

I got a certificate stamped by Uncle Sam, footprint and all.
Old Uncle Abe says we're citizens of a nation and a state.
So I pondered what Abe opined and to know what he saw,
Then I realized he was really on to something quite great,

On one hand I'm a citizen of Carolina, the state I claim,
And a citizen of the Texas Republic by treaty and tradition,
And simultaneously a citizen of the Unites States I remain,
So, I find myself as a trifecta citizen in a unique position.

A man without a country, thank God, I no longer be,
But of the USA, Carolina and Texas; a citizen of all three!

I Want My Country Back

I clicked off the news and looked at the screen with a stare,
Resisting the urge to fly into rage or sink into utter despair.

A sexagenarian American, I remember a time,
When the news was a useful and a necessary thing,

That was the last century, this is the 21st now who knows
What nonsense and useless information next they'll bring.

From cookie cutter locals to national bubbles,
They all sound like they are from some other planet.

In the beginning, the 4th estate existed to serve the people,
Now we the people serve their sponsors gambit.

But, nary a word to serve the needs of our great Republic,
Their gatekeepers self-serving minds must be set in granite.

The American Constitution, Puritan work ethic, the
Pioneer's spirit and self reliance are now taboo and gone,

The New World spirit made individuals proud and free,
But now the Liberty Bell can no longer sing our song.

The people's sweat equity, motivation and drive built
Something from nothing by hard work, hope and a prayer.

And turned nothing to wealth with the help of a God,
Now that they've got theirs they really no longer care.

The nation's perseverance is no longer valued by them,
Not their agenda but not too proud to cash in on their share.

We melded diverse groups who combined diverse values,
And created the unique American mind.

Now they try to expunge individualism and the American,
Spirit with a strange One World globalist kind.

So now, it looks like the news in the minority is majoring
On the minors to ignore the wishes of the popular majority?

And they do it with a license granted to them by the same?
To recall the license of a few by the majority our priority!

Perhaps it must be to let information flow free and,
Preserve the Republic we dearly love and know,

And let the multinationals go somewhere far from here,
Make their money overseas with their dog and pony shows.

###

Follies

A Black Friday Nightmare

Tick...tick...tick...tick...the wall clock snapped off the final seconds until the doors would be unlocked and the 1/2 price off before Christmas sale in Dohickey's Department Store would be on.

Trembling nervously, l crouched down behind the counter with the department manager, both of us armed with cash registers and rain checks. As l squatted on the hard cold floor l thought of all the packages and Christmases I had as a little boy on the farm.

l could remember the warmth that radiated from the embers of the fireplace as l sat and played with my new toys on Christmas day. Santa Claus was always good to me on Christmas even though my parents would always forlornly say, "Don't you expect much this Christmas."

Yet, once in awhile in my innocence l wondered where all the gifts came from or why my parents were so anxious to see if l was satisfied with each and every present. If only l knew what l know now.

Growing up, l ventured out more often and discovered the world of the toy stores and later the shopping mall. l watched the people, year after year, going in and coming out with armfuls of packages. Before long I discovered that Santa Claus was just a cover up for the sin of Christmas shopping.

Since then, l graduated to the front lines working right behind the counter in the notorious "department store." l watched thousands of crazed shoppers storm the counters and seize the displays in every department of the store. Speak of frantic perils, I've been around to see everything from fat ladies sizing pantyhose to fitting slippers for dogs. Also I was there the day they had the pie fight in the bakery and when the ladies room flooded with Mr. Bubble.

It was hard for me to look in the smiling, happy faces of my parents on Christmas Day and picture them out ruthlessly shopping, shouting, and running over people, but also l suppose they did for there was always a pile of presents under the tree. Needless to say, the cold facts have long since shattered my child-like innocence. And to think they were always such good Christians, well experience has taught me well.

What was that?...could it be?...yes, that was the click of the front door lock. It'll be only a matter of seconds now! Hastily, l finished my coffee and locked the door to the register booth.

In the distance l could detect a low, faint, rumbling noise which grew slowly like the waves of the mounting surf that picks up speed as it hurries to dash itself against the rocks. Closer and louder became the sound until it was now a dull roar. Mixed in with the uproar was the distinct trudge of shod feet and animal-like shrieks; onward it came.

Then, with a crash of breaking glass and a giant boom, the legions burst into our department. Instantly I jumped to my register keys. The scene was like a whirlwind of limbs and syllables and flying objects; total chaos for several moments that seemed like an eternity.

When I regained consciousness, I found myself half buried under a pile of Tonka trucks behind the counter. Half dazed, I beheld a scene of mass destruction and total desolation.

Venturing a peep over the edge of the counter l spied the second wave make the corner into the hall from the garden department. My department was next.

Closer, closer they came, pounding down the passage, waving arms and shouting "Viva la sale; viva la sale!" Sweat broke out on my forehead as l unlocked my register and tightened my tie. Now there were just a few yards of unbroken tile between the hoards and our position. My boss pulled out the new "Charge-a-plan" for reinforcement. He chewed on the end of his cigar violently.

Wham!!! In the wall of the counter a gaping hole appeared like a giant fist had ripped it open. l heard the moans of the stragglers of the horde sprawled on the floor.

But l was alive! I could hardly believe it. My boss, who l found lying limp across the counter was alive too. l was amazed. How could this be? I soon found out.

Turning around l soon discovered that the path of destruction came in and went through our counter and on into the department behind. And, there, I saw the grisly answer among the heaps of bodies and the smoke. Dangling half-destroyed from the ceiling was a tattered banner proclaiming "2/3 off price Christmas sale"….what a way to go!!!

Eggo Ego

Psychiatrist: "Tell me, 800373 what started you on a life of crime?"

Convict: "My name is Kikester, Mister Kikester, not 800373."

Psychiatrist: "Alright, Mr Kikester, tell me....."

Convict: "Let me tell you how I got started on a life of crime. A long, long time ago when I was a kid, and not very old, I had my first Easter. That Easter my mother came in my room with it, and from then on it was love at first sight.....my very first egg. I can still see its glimmering array of colors and design. It was lovely."

"My destiny was set. I remember my first Easter egg hunt, scrambling, searching and collecting those precious delicacies. Life was good then. I had my egg collection and lived quite contentedly for a good while, enjoying the life of leisure. But, little did I know or realize the diabolical scheming that was going on behind closed doors. I was naive to the evil that lurked in the corners."

"Then, one day fate dealt a shocking blow to my life! I was sitting at the table eating my poached eggs and reading the newspaper when I saw this headline, 'Egg Shortage Predicted.' I fell out of my chair in disbelief. Along with my wife I read the article which said the government was going to ban personal consumption of eggs, because of the shortage of eggs and run-on substitute artificial eggs. Both of us wept in deep sorrow. But, while my eyes were still wet I had resolved to fight back! Outlaw eggs? That was the last straw!"

"Together, with other like-minded connoisseurs and lovers of the 'real thing', we organized a resistance movement called the 'Egg Heads.' Immediately, we began to stock pile eggs, accumulate arms and formulate our plans. With a little research we found who the real culprits were.

We discovered that the sinister madman behind it went by the alias as one 'Colonel Sanders'. We surmised, being a military man, he used his connections with the government to work out a deal to promote fried chicken. Together with a man named 'MacDonald' they were killing off the chickens on one hand and on the other wiping out the few eggs that were available. And, as we suspected, their underlying motive was capitalism. Helping these devils, the government spread propaganda out to the people about the cholesterol in eggs saying they were harmful in an attempt to get people to stop eating them."

"That was all we could stand. The hour of decision was at hand! It was time to fight back and so we did. We began our attack by 'shelling' every fried chicken establishment on the map. All was going well for us, then those villains caught up with us. They cleverly concealed a cadre of soldiers inside a giant egg, They deceived us. In our joy we took the giant egg. We foolishly took it back to our chicken farm. We shattered the shell and a yolk of soldiers pounced upon us."

"And so now, here l am in the state prison manufacturing artificial eggs.'"

Psychiatrist: "So the egg has been a major influence over your life since childhood, l assume?"

Convict: "Egg-zactlyl"

###

La Telephone Fatale

Setting: (The scene is an isolated spot on a side walk somewhere in an unnamed city. A post-mounted payphone, rear-center of sidewalk and a bottle of wine are the only props.)

Cast: Two men. (1) A nameless wino and bum, (2) a nameless priest in full clergy dress.

Directions: (Scene opens, the wino is leaning against side canopy of phone, apparently asleep but still managing to hold onto the bottle in one hand. Enter the priest hurriedly from stage left towards the phone.)

Priest: (Reaching into his pocket for change) "At last a phone! I must call the Bishop and explain I'm late for the Cardinal's reception because I missed that bus!"

(Suddenly the wino sputters to life, oblivious to the priest's approach, slips around to the receiver and starts putting in coins. That brings the priest to an abrupt halt.)

Priest: (Wringing his hands, starts pacing impatiently) "Brother, please hurry."

Wino: (With back to priest, fumbles and drops a coin) "What's ya hurry, Rome wazin built in a day! Ah, hey, who ya callin' ya bwouther anyway?" (Wino stoops, pivots to pickup the coin, straightens and comes eye to eye with priest, pauses the continues) "Wha, wha, well, I didn't know I'ze whint all da way to Italy! That express bus sur is fast. I, ah musta slept plum thru the stop at Florence, Mississippi!?" (He scratches his head, bewildered)

Priest: "Could you please hurry? I need to contact the Bishop as quickly as possible."

Wino: (Belches accidentally, then winks at priest) "Hey! Ya seem like ya in sum kinda twouble?" (Suddenly pats the priest on the shoulder) "But, that's OK, ya can tell good ol' Charlie. I wudin tell a soul" (Puts hand over his heart and whispers) "I swear!"

Priest: (Impatiently starts pacing to and fro) " PLEASE! Would you just hurry, Sir?"

Wino: (Putting coins into phone and dialing) "Hewwo? Operator? I wanna call the United Staes." (Pauses, looking puzzled) "Whaata ya mean, it's the United States? Donya get smart with me!"

Priest: (Now totally exasperated, turns to audience, looks up and makes a silent prayer)
"Please hurry. I'm in a lot of trouble already!"

Wino: " HOLD onto ya collar. Ya ain the only one that's got a cross to bear!" (He hiccups and starts speaking into the receiver) " I wanna call Florence. No! I'm already in Italy! Oh, yeah? Same to ya, ya ungrateful heifer. Huh? Doin ya be talkin bout ma mhutter that way. Ya put me thru or I'm callin' Maw Bell haself, ya hear? Yeah, Florence, Mississippi, of the U. S. of A., got that? O.K."

(Wino waits on the phone, the priests, pacing, wipes his brow)
Wino: "Yeah? Uh huh? (Glances at the priest) "Well, he's right here. Ya wanna talk to HIM!?"

(The priest finally loses control, snatches the receiver and jerks it away from the wino's ear.)

Priest: "LOOK! I've had all I can stand. Gimme the phone, take a hike, jump in the lake, I don't care! Just shut up, OK ?"

(Priest slams receiver unto the hook, but the phone rings again instantly. The wino picks it up first.)

Wino: " Hewwo? (Stares at the priest amazed) "How did ya know? It' fe you! Someone named John Paul, err, somin'. Es he's the Pop."

(Wino hands phone to priest and exits Stage Left staggering)

Priest: "Hello? Yes? Yes? Oh...your Holiness!"

(Suddenly with a pop and a cloud of smoke the phone zaps the priest and he falls dead instantly)

(Suddenly the Wino returns to Center Stage looks at the priest for moment and then turns to face audience.)

Wino: (To audience) "I guess his impatience was killing him?!!"

(Curtains)

THE END

The Rebuke of Gog: A One Act Play

Prologue: This is a one act play. All activity centers around a bench in the common area of the local university.

The characters:

Gog: The proverbial street-wise thug with an ambition to exploit the innocent and unwary student. He is a student.

The Student: A college student who is haplessly at the center of the actions of the other two characters, presumably a freshman.

Apollo: An amiable loving soul who is an older more experienced student like Gog. Apollo's motives are altruistic and benevolent. Gog's are self-serving and assuming.

Setting: The Student is seated on the bench all the time reading or minding his own business. Apollo is Stage Left a few yards away from the bench. Gog enters from Center Front headed direct for the Student and ignoring Apollo.

Scene 1

Gog: "Hey... hi there. How are you doing? You new around here?"

Student "Oh,... kinda sorta."

Gog: "This your first time here?"

Student: "Ah... actually it's my second week."

Gog: "Mind if I sit down?" (Doesn't wait for answer, sits by student on the bench) "Well, I bet you'd like someone who's experienced around here like me to show you the ropes?"

Student: "I guess so..."

Gog: "Bet you need to make some money to support yourself too?"

Student: "Well I have a job at the campus bookstore."

Gog: "Yeah, that pays peanuts. Listen, let me tell you something really important, sorta secret." (Puts his arm around student's shoulder) "How would you like to make $100 an hour or so?"

Student: "Well.. sure. But how?" (Apollo moves closer to Student's right, eavesdropping.)

Gog: "Weeelll, its like this, you'll be taking tests here at school and like anyone else you get grades on them. All you got to do is figure out a way to get me the tests with the answers and I'll pay you $100 for each one you bring me. Cash! That's all there is to it."

Apollo: (Clearing throat & interrupting uninvited) "Hey, don't listen to him." (The Student stares at Apollo and then back to Gog speechless.)

Gog: "Don't listen to him. He's a fool!"

Apollo: "Not fool enough to risk being thrown out of school! Why don't you just get out of here and leave him alone." (Puts his arm around the Student who is in confused shock about all.)

Gog: (Rises, exits Stage Right) "Hey, kid if you want to make some good money don't listen to that clown. I'll see you later."

Scene 2

(Setting same as before)

Gog: "Hey kid. Good to see you again. What you reading?" (Keeps talking over Student) "Oh forget that boring stuff. Ya making any money?"

Student: "Not really..."

Gog: (Turns aside pulls out $100 bills and flashes them in Student's face.) "Looky, looky here what I got. Ya like that kid?" (Continues without allowing answer) "Like I said before, wouldn't you like to make some real money like this?"

Student: (Blurts out) "Well, I really need to make some money to pay for my books. If I don't get 'em soon I'll start flunking out and waste everything!"

Apollo: (Oblivious to the Student's point and need, focusing only on Gog) "Up to new tricks, huh, snake? You don't care about anyone. All YOU care about is money?"

Student: (Still seated as others ignore him and stands face to face behind the bench) "I lost my job, I need some money."

Gog: (Rising in vexation to Apollo) "Yer interruptin' my conversation. I can't stand it when people won't show you no respect in this world. Mind yer own bizzznus and shut your mouth before I shut it for YOU!" (Threatens with fist)

Apollo: (Pulls out cash and waves in the air distractedly) "What you really want is right here. Tell you what, if you'll leave 'em alone you can have whatever is here" (Pokes money in front of Gog)

Gog: (Grabs money, starts counting) "Oh yeah?" (Turns walking off Stage Right counting) "SUCKER!"

Apollo: (Turns to exit Stage Left, pats Student's shoulder and walks off) "Everything is alright. Everything is gonna be okay."

Student: (Sits alone on stage face in hands weeping).

Scene 3

(Setting same as before. Enter Gog Front Center stage, stopping momentarily with hands on hip glaring at student who is reading.)

Gog: (Stomps over to Student and slaps book shut) "Look! Look at me when I am talking to you here? I'm tired of fooling around with you." (Points finger right in Student's face and then shakes him by both shoulders,) "I'm tired of asking ya and now I'm telling ya, if ya know what is good for you you'll do as I say and get movin' on them tests. Ya understand me?" (Towering over Student, hands back on hips)

Apollo: (Runs over behind the bench) "Hey! Leave him alone, snake face!"

Gog: (Runs behind bench to confront Apollo) "Get lost loser!" (Shoves Apollo in the chest area.)

Apollo: "I'm tired of you picking on people. You don't have to bully 'em to get 'em to do what you want." (Shoves Gog back and a violent scuffle ensues. They are shouting incoherently and shoving each other,

(Gog turns and runs off Stage Right & Apollo turns and runs off Stage Left.)

Student: (Stands alone at the bench with arms spread in both directions and looks directly at audience) "I need the money! All I need is some money!"

(Curtains)

THE END

NFL Super Bowl Ad Contest Submission
© - 2006- Rick Dail

Setting: The time is 100 AD. The place is the Roman Colosseum

Scene 1

Shot 1: The Emperor is in stands with his female entourage and holds NFL Super Bowl ring up for the crowd to cheer.

Shot 2: The line of scrimmage on the gridiron with the Legionaries on one side and the Barbarians on the other side.

Shot 3: The Empress shows the football and throws it out onto the field.

Shot 4: The Legionaries present shields all up and down the line of scrimmage.

Announcer: "Football is about sacrifice!"

Shot: The Barbarian line parts showing a battering ram with a man riding on the ram rail carrying the ball.

Shot 5: Battering ram collides with shields and the ball carrier gets catapulted over the line of shields.

Shot 6: The ball carrier lands on his feet behind the line.

Announcer: "… AND overcoming adversity!"

Shot 6: Crowd roars and hurls fruits and vegetables down on the ball carrier.

Scene 2

Shot 1: Ball carrier is running towards goal and is confronted with a trench of burning oil.

Announcer: "It tests character…"

Shot 2: Ball carrier covers his face, leaps over through the flames. And runs to the end zone.

Announcer: "And those who pass the test…"

Shot 3: Ball carrier runs and leaps on top of wall and hands the football to the Emperor.

Announcer: ",,,Rise to the occasion and receive the glory!"

Shot 4: The Emperor hands the ring to ball carrier who still on wall holds it up for the crowd.

Announcer: "And those who don't … wait for another season!"

Shot 5: Emperor holds out hand gives the thumbs down gesture. Trap door opens on the field and the Legionaries fall through the space out of sight.

Announcer: "In the NFL the tradition continues!"

End

Reflection

The Park

It's hot. The kind of subtropical heat that makes your breath feel heavier than air. The white cement pavilion reflects the sunlight with blinding intensity. Its four corners drape over the picnic tables and touch the concrete like a gigantic stingray overpowering its prey. The drab green tables stretch out in five parallel rows underneath the canopy of cool cement. It's cool, only under the canopy's protective shroud. And there, a faint wisp of a Gulf breeze tickles your face like a feather,then disappears.

Under the dome of concrete the din assaults your ears. In the background the thud of an irritating beat of some nameless tune spills out of a boom box in the background, 30 to 40 feet away. In between, the endless drone of a hundred different voices in a cacophony of broken conversations hits your ears in waves. A shriek here a cackling laugh over there; pierce the air and your eardrums. It sounds like a picnic.

The crowd is a swirl of colors and dressed in a kaleidoscope of summer apparel. Some wear sandals, some sneakers, some with hats like rejects from a golf tournament, almost all with shorts in every imaginable shade of blue denim. You feel casual and relaxed. Yet the crowd stares from faces in pitch black lenses of sunglasses make you feel like you are in the presence of aliens. Nevertheless, the hum continues as people swarm to and fro all over the pavilion. They engage in close face-to-face encounters briefly them buzz off in every direction like bees. They go round and round the tables, standing here and sitting there, engaged in some unspoken game of musical chairs.

The blare of a megaphone barks out orders in an unintelligible language and groups scatter out from under the canopy. Some remain oblivious to the obnoxious interruption. It looks like a picnic.

In between the tables and groups, stretches of brownish weathered concrete sport occasional straw wrappers and scattered puddles of ominous looking liquid. Spilled drinks perhaps? The old concrete is laced with intricate patterns of cracks that resemble something like Martian canals crisscrossing it with abandon, without rhyme or reason. A few ugly cigarette buttes are scattered across the concrete. They look like squashed bugs, lifeless and dead. It is a picnic.

On the table in front of me the paper flutters in the breeze and I have to restrain it with both hands. I keep writing somber and serious with as much detachment as I can muster. A woman runs behind me to avoid the attack of a savage water gun assailant. Suddenly I am interrupted as I am converted into a human shield for her. Swish, a spray of cold-water droplets rushes over my head and some drops splash my face. They feel cool like fresh raindrops. Some land on my paper. The dual runoff just as suddenly as they appeared. I continue writing.

To the left a group of young women slouch on a bench of a picnic table snickering in a distracting way as one of them has endowed her tank top with two water-balloons to look like Dolly Parton. Then the water gun bandit returns, streaks across form left to right, confronting the women with a hail of droplet spray. The women scatter in all directions like a covey of quail invaded by a hunter.

At last some one turns down the boom box. As it's squawking declines, so does the din of the crowd. Conversations no longer have to be conducted at a shout. What a relief! The pressure melts from my eardrums.

"What are you doing? What are you studying?" Demands a passer by looking down at me with a perplexed grimace. "Homework!" I reply trying not to engage in any lengthy trivial dialogue. A few more questions are answered and the curious gaze appears appeased, and off the man goes to leave me to my toil.

Splat, a blue water balloon crashes on the table nearby. Fortunately, it missed the paper but did manage to break my concentration. It's followed by the sudden appearance of a female companion who plops at the bench on the other side of the table. She buffets me with a rapid series of inquiries about what I am doing and why. She confronts me with a trim rigid jaw and steel blue intense gaze. Looking and answering, I see a dark tanned, Arian face, without the slightest hint of dryness. The face looks like it was brushed on a canvas. I see no flaw. Her lips are tight and thin. I feel a flush of relief as she pulls back from being within inches of my face. Her questions answered, she turns to go almost as quickly as she came.

Off she goes to join the group who are out on the lawn to play volleyball. The group languishes in the intense sunlight moving with guarded motions, standing listlessly to conserve their energy. The white sphere of the volleyball goes back and forth over and over the rusted uprights and net. Its journey is lazy and monotonous. Occasionally it peels off out of sight on a botched serve. The players dutifully rotate around the court and periodically emit a burst of glee and clap of hands. Most of the time, they just seem to patiently endure the relentless heat.

The woman in the group with shoulder length brown hair turns her head as a gust blows her locks from shoulder to shoulder. She manages to continue the conversation with her companion without the locks slapping her face. Apparently the group gets a burst of wind now and then to relieve the stifling thick air on the court.

Under the shade of the canopy the same breeze feels like the residue from a cooling fan rather than a blast from a furnace. I suddenly realize how much I appreciate the difference a little shade can make. I continue writing.

Slowly but surely, I sense growing pains under my thighs. A dull burning sensation. It's the pain of sitting on the hard plank bench seat for too long. I feel the sticky moisture of sweat between my skin and the blue jeans underneath. A wiggle brings a temporary rush of relief over my lower extremities, but just moments later the numbness returns. Sitting is becoming a test of endurance. Then I slowly become aware that a strange pain is spreading from my wrist into the plantar aspect of my right hand. The fingers begin to twinge in pain. Flexing the fingers does not bring any relief. They almost spasm in rebellion to my tight grip on the pen. They are talking to me in a language too complex for words. I have been writing too long. Beads of sweat appear on my brow like condensation.

Now a black fly with a grotesque torso lights on the table. It marches straight for my paper. A flick of the forearm shoos him off but in a moment he is back again. Another lightning sweep of the arm sends him away again, but as soon as I turn my gaze in another direction he's right back more defiant than ever. A heavy sigh escapes my nostrils showing my own mounting frustration.

Automatically I chuck the pen and stand up as if my muscles have taken over command from my mind. A freshness runs up and down my spine and legs. I now see I have been writing too long. My right hand ceases its protests. Enough is enough.

I leave for the inviting air conditioning of my automobile. The door shuts, the noise fades into nothingness and my central nervous system is soothed by the silence. It was a picnic. Its over now. Now, it's time to go home.

###

Tribute to Ida Bell
(Excerpts from mother's eulogy 2012)

Thank you for coming today on this special occasion. Please forebear with me as I do not do much public speaking:

Name

There was no one like Ida Bell. There was no one like Ida Bell Slay Dail Motley and I was proud to call her "Mamma". There was no one like Ida Bell and there will never, ever be anyone like her again.

Slay Family

Actually there never could be. She was a product of her times and lineage. Born to the Slays, a humble, resilient hardworking line of people that first migrated to America in the 1650s, and, eventually migrated across the South to Texas in the 1850s.

They were a hardworking, resourceful and practical sort of folk who relied on faith and a great sense of humor to weather the trials and storms of life. They struck out for the frontier to find opportunity and freedom and a future for themselves and their families. Mother was molded and tempered by those same elements.

Orphaned at age nine in the midst of the Great Depression, beset with the meager fare of rural Texas existence in those days, she set out as a teenager, virtually alone, to Washington D. C. during The War to make a new life for herself. And, that she did.

Mamma's Values

She had four rowdy boys and raised them as best she could, surviving two husbands in the process. Never mind that she did not have money or education or insurance; Mamma always persevered and provided what we needed to the best of her abilities. No one could cook fried chicken like Mamma and her banana pudding has yet to be matched. On a cold snowy night, Mamma could make a batch of navy beans and cornbread fit for a king to satisfy her ravenous sons.

What Mamma could not provide in material means she far surpassed with her values and wisdom. She taught us to wash dishes, mop the floors, make the bed and wash our clothes in that evil Maytag ringer washing machine. Lord, you know I hated ironing clothes!

Mamma we remember.

You taught us that money wasn't everything in life. You made us go to Church when we didn't want to in order to teach spiritual values and truth. You taught us to mind our manners when we had company, be respectful of elders and to be grateful for whatever we received. You taught us to dry our clothes out on the radiator on wintry nights and how to take care of what we had. You taught us that if we have clean clothes, a clean body and a clean heart we were just as good as the next man. And to be proud of who we are. Mamma taught us to value honesty and good character. She taught us to say grace, and that if we wanted anything, the value of working for it.

By example she showed us to seek our value not in the type of work we did but, instead, what kind of person we were. She tried her best to show what a man is when there was no father to turn to. Her house was always an oasis of peace from a hectic and stressful World outside, a haven of rest.

Mamma was good-hearted almost to a fault. She would do just about anything to help out her boys when it was really needed. I will never forget the time she showed up in the middle of the night to bail me out of jail with her own money when I deserved to be there.

Mamma I remember!

What Mamma Said

Although Mamma only had a Tenth grade education she had an awful lot of wisdom. She always said "You've got to make do the best you can."I will never forget when my life hit rock bottom and Mamma said over and over again, "Rickey, you've got to move on." She taught us that life is not always fair and taught us to trust in God. She said things like "their day will come". Mamma said you have to forgive and forget. She always said she could "read people like a book" and nine times out of ten she was right.

Mamma taught us to stick_together and to watch out for each other, to think for ourselves and not to be afraid to stand by our opinions. Mamma, said "Its got to get dark before it'll lighten up".

Mamma we remember!

You sure were right about that too. She taught us to reverence the Word and to love Gospel music.
And, she used to say, "You can do anything you set your mind to." I am still working on that one Mamma!

Mamma's Legacy

My Mamma, Ida Bell, never had a lot of worldly goods or wealth or material things to leave behind, but she left us with wonderful memories, great values, a love for God and an example of character and integrity that we can only hope to live up to. Those are the priceless things and we are so grateful for that. She also left four sons, all of whom have been blessed with a college education, ten grand children who always sparked a twinkle in her lovely blue eyes and three great-grand-children as a down payment for the future. She also influenced five daughter-in-laws whom she loved like her own, no matter what.

The Long Road Home

For twenty plus years Mamma said she "was ready to go home." Only, it did pan out quite that way. It seems God had a lot more people for Mamma to meet and influence and bless before He was ready to bring her on home. And that Mamma also did.

Mamma used to tell me that "People were the most interesting subject under the sun." I believe she was right. Mamma was strong. And, despite the fact that the last years of her journey became increasingly difficult and hard, Mamma was still touching hearts and souls in her unique, whimsical ways, and charming folks almost up to the last weekend of her life. And now it's over. The long road has ended. The race is finished. The trials are over.

There will be no more physical maladies and no more tears, for you are home at last. You are in the care of Jesus, the one who loves you more than we possibly ever could, and reunited with your mamma whom you lost at the tender age of three. And for this reason, we rejoice for you despite our loss here. And we will forever be blessed by your legacy and memory. God's blessings of peace and rest and joy on you.

And we remember Mamma...always!

Thank you.

www.ingramcontent.com/pod-product-compliance
Lightning Source LLC
Chambersburg PA
CBHW072130150726
47999CB00005B/2227